W9-AQO-563

Strudel Stories

OTHER YEARLING BOOKS YOU WILL ENJOY:

A LETTER TO MRS. ROOSEVELT, C. Coco De Young
THREE AGAINST THE TIDE, D. Anne Love
BESS'S LOG CABIN QUILT, D. Anne Love
SUMMER SOLDIERS, Susan Hart Lindquist
THE WOLVES OF WILLOUGHBY CHASE, Joan Aiken
DANGEROUS GAMES, Joan Aiken
THE RUNAWAYS, Zilpha Keatley Snyder
GIB RIDES HOME, Zilpha Keatley Snyder
IF I FORGET, YOU REMEMBER, Carol Lynch Williams
THE COOKCAMP, Gary Paulsen

YEARLING BOOKS are designed especially to entertain and enlighten young people. Patricia Reilly Giff, consultant to this series, received her bachelor's degree from Marymount College and a master's degree in history from St. John's University. She holds a Professional Diploma in Reading and a Doctorate of Humane Letters from Hofstra University. She was a teacher and reading consultant for many years, and is the author of numerous books for young readers.

Strudel Stories

Joanne Rocklin

A YEARLING BOOK

JF Rocklin
Rocklin, Joanne.   SEP 0 7 '12
Strudel stories

by
DELL YEARLING
an imprint of
Random House Children's Books
a division of Random House, Inc.
1540 Broadway
New York, New York 10036

If you purchased this book without a cover you should be aware that this book is stolen property. It was reported as "unsold and destroyed" to the publisher and neither the author nor the publisher has received any payment for this "stripped book."

Copyright © 1999 by Joanne Rocklin

Strudel recipe on page 123:
"Back to Basics: Shortcut Strudel" by Joan Drake
Copyright © 1997, *Los Angeles Times*. Reprinted by permission.

All rights reserved. No part of this book may be reproduced or transmitted in any form or by any means, electronic or mechanical, including photocopying, recording, or by any information storage and retrieval system, without the written permission of the Publisher, except where permitted by law. For information address Delacorte Press, 1540 Broadway, New York, New York 10036.

The trademarks Yearling® and Dell® are registered in the U.S. Patent and Trademark Office and in other countries.

Fans can visit Joanne Rocklin at her Web site! www.geocities.com/Athens/Delphi/5464

Visit us on the Web! www.randomhouse.com/kids

Educators and librarians, for a variety of teaching tools, visit us at www.randomhouse.com/teachers

ISBN: 0-440-41509-8

Reprinted by arrangement with Delacorte Press

Printed in the United States of America

August 2000

10 9 8 7 6 5 4 3 2 1

OPM

In loving memory of my grandparents

ANNA SIEGAL SANDLER

LOUIS SANDLER

SLAVA CHERNIKOFF ROCKLIN

ISRAEL ROCKLIN

Acknowledgments

I AM VERY GRATEFUL TO THE FOLLOWING people and organizations for their assistance and inspiration during the creation of this book:

Rosalie Abel; Rupa Basu; Madeleine Comora; Marjorie Cowley; Jeffrey Dosik, Barry Moreno, and the Ellis Island Immigration Museum Library; Karen Gaiger; Kristine O'Connell George; Paula Gerson; Monica Gunning; Joan Hewett; Ann Shore and the Hidden Child Foundation–Anti-Defamation League; Sarah Jackson; Judith Kancigor; Isidore Kulkin; Irwin Levinson, M.D.; Nancy Smiler Levinson; Sonia Levitin; Hava BenZvi, Sally Hyman, and the Los Angeles Jewish Community Library; the Lower East Side Tenement Museum; Esther Morgenstern; Joan Nathan; Bertha Nelson; Gerald Nelson; Ann Whitford Paul; Ronald Paul, M.D.; Adele and Hyman Rocklin; Ellen Rocklin; June Salander; Miriam Schwartz; Eric Silverberg; Michael Silverberg; Erica Silverman; Amalia Dembitzer-Levin and Adaire Klein, Director of Library and Archival Services, and the Simon Wiesenthal Center and Museum of Tolerance; Marie Lore and the South Street Seaport Museum; Robert Sturtz; and Vicki Zack.

To Ruth Cohen and Laura Hornik, a special thank-you.

Contents

Strudel
Stories

GRANDPA WILLY DIED THE DAY AFTER the Los Angeles Dodgers pulled off a triple play. My older sister, Jessica, and I had watched the game with him, the three of us propped up on pillows in his hospital bed. I loved my grandpa very much. All during the funeral, I waited for my tears to come. But those tears had turned hard inside my chest, like a big old baseball I'd swallowed by mistake.

Afterwards, relatives and friends came to our house for the *shivah*. They would come all that week, carrying platters of food, to help us mourn.

"What a terrific ball game Willy got to see before he died!" said Great-uncle Dave, filling his plate with desserts. "He always had such great timing."

"That's a terrible thing to say!" I snapped.

Startled, Great-uncle Dave dropped a piece of cherry strudel onto his lap.

"Oh, Lori, Dave didn't mean anything unkind," said my mother. She put her arms around me. "It's been such a hard day. You're upset."

"It was only a joke, kid," said my great-uncle kindly.

"I know," I said, my voice muffled against my mother's shoulder. The baseball inside me felt bigger than ever. "Still, do you make jokes and laugh and whoop it up on the day of someone's funeral? Someone you loved very, very much?"

"Well, yes, you do," said my sister, Jessica. "I mean, you *can*. Grandpa would have."

She was right, of course. Grandpa Willy would have laughed—for lots of reasons:

Because the strudel from the deli tasted like cherries on cardboard.

Because my cousin Sandy's baby was so funny and sweet.

Because Great-uncle Dave was wearing a new toupee, a bit lopsided under his *yarmulke*.

And because, yes, Grandpa's timing *had* been great.

One week later I heard noises in the kitchen. The sun wasn't up yet. I went downstairs to investigate.

Standing at the counter, his back to me, was Grandpa Willy's ghost! Same baseball cap turned backward, same green apron, same long legs in faded jeans. The ghost was stirring something in a bowl.

"Grab a knife and peel those apples on the table," Jessica said.

"Oh, it's you," I said. Shaking, I sat down. "For a second, I thought . . ."

"What?" Jessica asked.

"Nothing," I said.

"You thought I was Grandpa, right?"

"Don't be a dork," I said. "Grandpa's dead."

And I started to cry. Finally.

"Hey," said Jessica softly. She handed me a crumpled tissue from her apron pocket.

I looked at it. "It's used."

"Sorry," said Jessica. She put her hand on my shoulder. "Want to hear a riddle?"

I blew my nose. "Not really."

"Come on! It was one of your faves when you were a little girl. Here it is: When is a baseball like a chicken?"

"I give up."

Jessica's sneakered feet did a little dance. *Slappity-tap!* She leaned forward with her arm outstretched, just like Grandpa used to do. "When it's a . . . ?"

"Foul," I said, smiling a little. But now I was crying harder than ever. The crying felt so good, like a gift from Grandpa himself. "Okay, so you're telling Grandpa's jokes and you're wearing his apron. I suppose you're making his strudel too?"

Jessica sat down beside me. "Right. I've got his recipe. Did you taste that disgusting cherry strudel at the *shivah*? It came from a deli. I tell you, Grandpa would have died." She looked at me quickly. "You know what I mean."

"I know what you mean," I said. "Of course, if we bake Grandpa's strudel we'll have to tell all the stories, all those old stories the other bakers told."

"Of course," Jessica said. "Without stories the strudel will be a big fat flop. Can't you just hear Grandpa saying that?"

"Of course we never believed him." I put the tissue in my bathrobe pocket and reached for an apple and the paring knife.

"Never," said Jessica. "But then again, why take a chance?"

We looked at each other and laughed.

Was it my imagination? A memory of other times? I was pretty sure I heard Grandpa Willy in that kitchen, laughing with us.

Sarah's Kitchen

———— 🍎 ————

*I*MAGINE A KITCHEN IN ODESSA, A Russian city by the Black Sea. The year is 1894.

"Now, Mama, now!" shouts Isaac. He stands on tiptoe, leaning against the big wooden table.

"Shush!" says his big sister, Hannah. She pokes him with her elbow. "You'll wake the baby!"

Sarah, their mother, is kneading flour, sugar, eggs, and water into a soft ball. "Patience, *kinderlach*," she says.

Kinderlach means "little children" in Yiddish. That is the language they are speaking.

"Now, Mama?" Isaac whispers.

His mother's hands move in the bowl. Suddenly, *slam!* Then *slam!* again and again. She has picked up the ball of dough and is slamming it hard against the tabletop.

"Hurrah!" shouts Isaac.

In her cradle by the huge white-tiled stove, the baby stirs.

Hannah picks her up, pointing to the big table. "Look, Bertha! Mama is making the dough nice and smooth for our strudel." She kisses Baby Bertha's round red cheek. Then she lays her down again, smoothing the blanket over the baby's shoulders.

"I counted one hundred slams upon the table," sings Isaac, who loves numbers. He also loves the letters of the Hebrew and Russian alphabets, which march like soldiers in his papa's books.

"One hundred. You are right," says his mother. She lays down the dough at last. "Now the dough must rest. It is time for you to rest too."

"I don't want to rest!" cries Isaac. He stamps

his foot. "I'm not a baby like Bertha. I am a big fellow! I am five years old!"

"Hah! Some big fellow!" says Hannah. With a sharp knife she begins to peel an apple for the strudel.

"I am a brave fellow too!" Isaac marches around the big table. *"Tum tara rum tum!* I will run away to bang the drum in the czar's army, I will!"

Hannah smiles mischievously. "But there's no strudel in the army."

Isaac stops marching. "No?"

"There is only gruel and sometimes roasted pig," says Hannah.

Then she deepens her voice to a teasing growl. "From the mouth of the wicked czar fire spews. Silver daggers fly from his eyes. And he gobbles up any child marching in his way."

Isaac's eyes are round. He scurries under the table. He holds his knees to make himself small.

"Hah! Some brave fellow!" says Hannah, laughing.

"Hannah! For shame, frightening your

brother like that!" cries her mother. "Where did you hear such childish nonsense?"

"From Beryl, the egg woman," says Hannah, her face red.

Her mother's mouth is a straight line. "Beryl, the egg woman, has straw where her brains should be! Isaac, come out and help Mama crack walnuts."

"I'm hiding from the czar," comes Isaac's muffled reply.

"We are here," his mother says. "The czar is far away."

"May his stomach swell and his pants fall down!" shouts Isaac from under the table.

Soon Isaac falls asleep in his hiding place. Sarah checks her recipe, words written in Yiddish on a small scrap of paper. Then Sarah and Hannah peel apples and crack walnuts. After a while, Sarah spreads a clean cloth over the table. It is embroidered with spidery vines and buds of periwinkle blue. She rolls out the strudel dough to make a big circle, a circle even bigger than Baby Bertha's blanket. Then Sarah slips both hands carefully, oh so carefully, under that circle. She begins to walk slowly around the table, stretching and stretching and *stretching* the dough until Hannah says:

"I see them, Mama!"

"I see them too!" cries Isaac, crawling out from under the table. "I saw them first! Before you, Hannah!"

The dough has become so thin that the children can see right through to the blue flowers and vines of the tablecloth. That means it is time to spread the dough with apples and nuts and cherry preserves and warm melted butter. Then their mother gently folds the dough, over and over, into a fat roll curved like a horseshoe. She places the roll on a pan, which she shoves into the great iron oven.

Then Sarah adds more water to the samovar for tea.

"Stories now, Mama?" Isaac asks.

Sarah nods and picks up her mending. Baby Bertha wakes up. Hannah, listening to her mother's stories, holds the baby on her knee. Isaac makes a tower on the floor with the walnut shells, listening too.

Sarah's stories enter the warm oven, smoothing the dough and sweetening the sugar. As the

strudel bakes, the stories tuck themselves between the apple slices. Later, when Hannah and
Isaac eat the strudel, it seems they can taste
those stories. Stories about Jonah, cheerfully
stepping from the belly of a whale. Stories about
Moses, striding the floor of the Red Sea.

And stories that grow from a question.

"Did your mama bake strudel when you were
a little girl?" Isaac asks.

"Ah," says Sarah, stirring cherry preserves
into her tea, "when I was a little girl . . ."

Sarah's Stories

The Boy Who Danced with Ghosts

WHEN I WAS A LITTLE GIRL I LIVED IN A poor market town, far away from Odessa. Hunger, not apple strudel, filled my stomach much of the time. My mama made strudel very seldom. But one apple strudel I remember well. To this day, nothing has ever tasted so delicious! A portion of heaven, that strudel was.

But before I can tell you about that glorious strudel, I must tell you two stories.

15

The first is about a boy who danced with ghosts. And lived to tell about it!

That boy was my younger brother, Eli. You are surprised, of course. I have never before spoken to you about a brother named Eli. Listen and you will soon understand.

My parents were betrothed before they were born. They met for the first time on their wedding day. My papa, your *zaideh* Yakov, was a smiling boy of seventeen, fuzz on his cheeks for a beard. And my mama, your *bubbe* Leah, was only fourteen.

Why so young, you may ask?

A married man would not have to join the army, where Jews were forced to forget the faith of their fathers. Papa did not want that to happen. And so he married my mama. Love grew between them. Soon I was born, and then with much feasting and dancing at his bedside, my brother, Eli.

Papa was not a coward, that he refused to fight for the czar. Once I saw Papa stare down a wild dog in our yard, until the dog blinked its yellow eyes and turned away. And Papa was not a weakling. He was a water carrier, as strong as they come. To and from the pump and the river, his broad back bore the heavy yoke with its pails. Papa sang as he worked, bringing water and a melody to all the housewives.

But one dry summer day a fire raged throughout the town, swallowing the little crooked houses in its path. Papa tried to help, bringing water in his pails. The smoke overwhelmed him. He died, they said, whispering for us. This was in 1872. I was seven years old, and little Eli, only five.

"Ah, Eli!" cried Mama. "You are now the only man in our home."

But my brother, Eli, was small and skinny, like a cucumber for pickling. His nose was always running and he shivered with cold in every season. Everything scared him—dogs, goats, birds, people. Even the wind whistling through our leaky roof at night.

"*Boo*, Eli!" the other children would shout as they ran by our yard.

And Eli, that man in our home, what did he do? He sniffled and shook. He hid behind Mama's skirts, or mine.

We were very poor. Mama sold bagels at a

market stall. I kneaded the dough at home, keeping an eye on Eli. We worked very hard. But often only a potato and a piece of fat floated in the Sabbath soup.

One day, when Eli was six years old, Mama said, "It is time for my only son to go to school."

"Mama!" I cried. "How will you pay Eli's teacher?"

Mama held up the brass Sabbath candlesticks. They had belonged to her mother, and her mother's mother before her.

"I will sell these candlesticks," she said. And Mama marched to the pawnshop that very day.

How I would have loved to go to school! Mama taught me how to read and write at home, but only in Yiddish. It was the boys who went to school to study the holy books of our fathers in Hebrew.

But did Eli leap for joy? Did he kiss Mama's hands and say, "Oh, Mama, thank you, thank you for sending me to school!"?

No, he did not.

"*Aieee! Aieee!*" shrieked Eli like a frightened chicken. Mama had to drag him through the village to the teacher's house.

He was afraid of the teacher, who had a bushy black beard and piercing eyes. He was afraid of the other students, noisy and bigger than he. He was even afraid of the alphabet! He would hide under the bench when it was his turn to read.

"Eli, Eli, Turnip Head!" sang the other boys, chasing him home.

"I hate school," Eli told Mama.

"Oh, Eli, what would your poor papa say?" she asked.

Eli hung his head in shame.

Several years later, the pale winter sun brought days colder than we'd ever known. And a terrible influenza arrived with the peddlers from Vilna. Many in our town died. Mama gave us glass after glass of pickle juice and foul-tasting oil. She fasted and prayed for our health.

But Eli, small and frail though nine years old, came down with that awful fever. His skin was hot and dry but he shivered under his blanket. We spread coats and pillows on top of the stove, and there we laid Eli, for greater warmth. Mama kept that oven burning day and night. She even split a bench for wood. Eli continued to shiver.

Wise elders brought medicines and herbs. Soon the rabbi came to recite psalms, and we were sure the end was near.

"Poor little Eli," said the rabbi.

Suddenly I, Sarah, knew just what to do!

I jumped up and stood at Eli's feet, pointing my finger at him. In a clear, loud voice I said, "See, Rabbi, how my brother *Yakov* sleeps? *Yakov* will wake up soon for a bite of cake. Then he will shout and chase the chickens in the yard. That's what my brother *Yakov* will do."

The rabbi looked puzzled. "I thought the boy's name was—"

My mama interrupted him. "Sarah is correct. *Yakov* will wake up soon."

You may ask why we changed our sick boy's name to Yakov, the very name of my dead papa. To fool the Angel of Death, that's why! He had come for a boy named Eli. He would find a boy named Yakov in his place.

Did I feel something flutter by my cheek that afternoon? Did I hear a disappointed sigh at the window? Did I really fool the angel? I wondered.

"Of course!" Eli, now Yakov, said later. "I saw the angel myself."

"What did he look like?" I asked.

"I can't remember, exactly," Eli/Yakov said. "Well, maybe he looked a little like Moishe the candlemaker, with his big ears and shiny forehead. Or maybe . . ." Eli/Yakov's voice trailed off. "You see, I wasn't really paying attention. I was much too busy dancing."

"Dancing! You didn't look like you were dancing, lying there so sick," I said.

Eli/Yakov's eyes shone. "Oh, yes! I danced for hours. I was at a big party in a great hall, at the entrance to heaven. What a feast we had! Chicken and fish and stewed pears. White bread, soft as a rich man's pillow. And, Sarah, all our dead relatives were at that party. Scholars! Healers! Circus performers! Men who could wrestle wild boars to the ground. I danced with them all."

"And Papa," I said. "He was at the party too, of course."

"And Papa." Eli/Yakov smiled and drew himself up tall. "Papa had been standing at the back.

He was carrying his water pails. But his yoke and the pails were made of gold. He waited until I finished dancing and eating before he came forward. He gave me a kiss and said, 'My name is your name now.' The angel scowled, disappearing into the darkness. Then Papa sang me a beautiful song as I leaned against his chest. And that's when I woke up."

When my brother had opened his eyes on his sickbed, he had said, "Mama, I brought you something from Papa." Then in a clear, sweet voice, he sang Papa's song.

Well, my mother fainted immediately into the rabbi's arms. When she came to, she said, "My son has the ghost of his papa inside him."

And that is how my brother (your uncle Yakov, whom you know well) danced with ghosts and lived to tell about it.

The Apple that Turned to Gold

NOW I COME TO MY SECOND STORY, ABOUT a forbidden apple tree. This tree's apples could turn to gold! It is also another story about my brother, Eli, now Yakov.

Yakov amazed us all with his remarkable recovery. In the next few years he grew strong and tall. He could run like a graceful pony. He could float on his back in the river for hours, balancing a book on his knee. And the book stayed dry.

Yakov became the leader of all the boys in town. "Hup! Hup!" he would shout, waving his wooden sword. "Forward, troops, to fight the enemy!" No boy at school ever teased him again.

And there's more. My brother, who once feared the alphabet, became a fine student. Every week, in front of the whole class, Yakov was given a special test. The teacher would choose one word from the Bible.

"Now, Yakov," the teacher would say. "Imagine that I am pushing a sharp pin through this word. Down, down goes the pin, until its head is flat against the page."

Yakov would close his eyes, imagining.

Then the teacher would ask, "Which words would the pin touch on all the other pages?"

Yakov could recite them all. It wasn't magic, but memory. Yakov could see every blessed word in his mind's eye. Perhaps you find this hard to believe, but it's true.

"Such a scholar, your Yakov!" crowed Mama's customers.

Were bagels tastier when baked by the family of Yakov the scholar? That can be argued. But customers bought more bagels than ever before. Now Mama could afford a little meat for our soup. We were less hungry.

Yet sometimes, even when the belly is full, there is another kind of hunger.

Now I will tell you about the forbidden apple tree. It grew wild, not in a Garden of Eden, but in a nobleman's forest beyond the bridge.

"You must not cross the bridge," Mama always said.

"Why not?" asked Yakov.

"Just do as I say, or else!" Mama warned. "It is dangerous to go where you are not welcome. There is hate beyond that bridge. There is hate everywhere we don't belong."

But Yakov had a hunger that grew and grew. He wanted to see more than the dusty town where we Jews were ordered by the czars to live. He began to read books in strange languages. He studied the stars. He spoke of deep oceans and cities with golden spires. What danger was there in crossing one little bridge?

So one warm Sabbath day in late summer, Yakov and I waited patiently. We did not remove our good Sabbath clothes. Mama's eyes drooped. Her head nodded. We waited until . . .

"Z-z-z-z-z-z!" Her snores filled up the house.

"Now," Yakov whispered.

Off we ran. At the far end of town, we stopped at the bridge and gazed at the shallow river flowing beneath.

"Part, Red Sea!" we shouted . . . and raced to freedom! Our shoes clattered across the bridge. We kept going, through dry wheat fields and wet pastures, toward a nobleman's forest, dark and unknown. At the forest's edge, we stopped.

There stood the apple tree, its fruit waiting. We gobbled up one, two, three apples each. It was the sweetest fruit we had ever tasted. Ah, it was like heaven. Then we lay down in the shade of the tree and spoke of our plans and wishes.

"When I am grown, I will read books and smoke cigars under my very own apple tree," said Yakov.

"And I will marry a scholar—like you, Yakov," I said. "I will eat white rolls at every meal and have seven Sabbath dresses to choose from."

Yakov was thoughtful for a few moments. Then he sat up. "I have two wonderful ideas," he said.

He broke off a twig from a branch. "A pen," he said.

He dipped the twig into the black juice of the rotting apples on the ground. "Ink. And this is our parchment," said Yakov, writing a Hebrew letter on a dead, dry leaf. "I will teach you the alphabet under this tree."

"And your second wonderful idea?" I asked.

Yakov grinned. "Would you believe me if I told you we can turn these apples into gold?"

"Of course I don't believe you," I answered.

"It's true, it's true," Yakov said. "We will turn the apples into gold."

My brother danced around the tree. He did a somersault or two. Then he flopped down beside me. "Well, maybe not gold. But what about brass?"

"How, then?" I asked. Yakov was so happy, I really did believe him. Yakov could do anything, I thought.

"First, I have a question," he said. "What does Mama use for Sabbath candlesticks?"

"The candles stand inside baked potatoes," I answered.

"And why aren't the candles held instead by two shiny brass candlesticks?" Yakov asked.

"Oh, Yakov," I said sadly. "You know why. Mama sold her candlesticks to Simon the pawnbroker."

"Listen," said Yakov. "We will pick apples and sell them to the fruit vendor. Then we will have money to buy candlesticks for Mama. And money left over to buy new boots for me. And for you, another holiday dress."

"Another!" I exclaimed, for I had only one, which I was wearing that day. "And what will we tell Mama?"

Of course Yakov had an answer for that too. "We will tell her we gathered goose feathers to sell. Or found a hidden treasure. Don't worry. We will think of something very clever."

I filled the skirt of my dress with apples. Yakov kicked off his boots and stuffed them to the brim. We would come back to pick apples again, we decided, and we planned all we would buy.

"Three warm coats."

"Books."

"A new goat."

"A cow."

Suddenly a whistle pierced the air. We whirled around. Racing toward us were a man and his snarling dog. The man's words, though not his accent, were of our language.

"Thieves! Thieves! Be off, you Jewish thieves!" he shouted. The dog barked angrily.

Apples tumbled onto the grass as I broke into a run.

"Come, Yakov," I shouted, glancing over my shoulder.

Yakov stood as still as the tree. He clutched his boots.

Pounding footsteps came closer and closer. I turned to see the man pick up a rock.

"Yakov!" I shouted again.

But still my brother didn't move. I raced back.

"Yakov, please!" I said, tugging at his arm.

I heard a small, sad sound from Yakov. Dropping his boots, he began to run. We fled like frightened ponies side by side, over the meadow to the bridge, and home. Never, ever had I run so fast!

"Where are your boots, your good Sabbath boots?" Mama demanded of Yakov.

Yakov told her about crossing the bridge. He told her about the apple tree, and the apples we'd picked. And the gift of the candlesticks she would never receive. Then he gave Mama the one apple he had carried home in his hand.

Mama frowned. "For shame! Working on the Sabbath! And those apples weren't yours to sell. You did not belong on that property."

"I know," whispered Yakov, hanging his head. He began to cry. I cried too.

So how did an apple turn to gold?

That night Mama baked us a gift: a golden strudel. A strudel baked with Mama's love and her forgiveness, and inside, sliced as thin as paper, Yakov's apple.

I have never tasted anything more delicious.

A Ghost for the Second Time

I MUST TELL YOU ONE MORE STORY.

Children, about most things my mama was right. About hate, sometimes she was wrong.

It was several years later. Yakov was thirteen. I am sure of his age. When the wheat still grew in the fields, he had been called to the altar for the first time, to read the blessed Torah. How proud he was to be a man!

In the dead of winter that year there came a storm I will never forget. The wind howled and hurled the snow against our windows.

At dawn Yakov put on our dead papa's coat, tied with a sash, and Papa's round fur cap.

"You can't go out on a day like this!" Mama cried.

"Hah! Is this a storm? A little breeze, a sprinkling of snow—nothing I've not faced before," Yakov boasted.

Off he went to morning prayer services.

The storm raged all day. Yakov did not return. Night fell. Anxiously, we waited. Yakov did not return that long, cold night, nor the next day. Men searched the snowbanks, beating them with sticks. Mama and I sat at the table, rocking back and forth, back and forth, already mourning.

But then there came a loud thumping at the door. A large peasant wearing leggings, tall boots, and a big bearskin hat stood at our threshold. On his back he had a sack of food for us: eggs, cabbages, loaves of bread. In his arms was Yakov wrapped in a sheepskin, alive, and with a smile on his lips.

The rest of this story was pieced together from what Yakov and this man, who spoke Polish with our mother, told us.

It seemed that, even for Yakov, the storm had been too fierce. Blinded by snow, he had trudged north instead of south, east instead of west. Nothing looked familiar. The wind swallowed up his shouts.

"But then," said Yakov, "out of that whirlwind there came a boy I did not know. He was crying, for he was lost too. We walked a long time, holding each other up. Finally we sank into a snowbank. Never have I felt so tired. But I knew that Papa's coat was warm—and surely big enough to cover us both. We had a very nice sleep, until his father found us."

A very nice sleep indeed! Rubbed with snow and rags, only the other boy awakened. Yakov, blue and still, was taken for dead. All night long, this gentile family cried for our Yakov, who, with his father's coat, had saved their child.

"The next morning, when I sat up and spoke," Yakov told us, "they thought there was a ghost before them. And, of course, I almost was a ghost, half-dead with cold. They wrapped me up and gave me barley soup and tea. And carried me home to you."

I burned to ask the most important questions of all.

"Oh, Yakov! When you were a ghost for the second time, did you dance? And did you see Papa, with his golden yoke and pails?"

"Of course," said Yakov. "Papa sends his love to all."

Thereafter, there was a bond between that Polish family and ours. One Passover, I remember, we shared matzos with their children, who taught us a game with painted eggs. But that is another story.

Sarah's Recipe

Bertie's Kitchen

OW, IMAGINE A KITCHEN IN Brooklyn, New York. The year is 1947. Willy, his sister, Irene, and their cousin Howie are visiting their great-aunt Bertie. And that's what Bertie is, they all agree. Great!

"Aunt Bertie, you have the best ideas," says Irene. "An apple strudel birthday cake."

It is Bertie's birthday and the children are helping her celebrate.

"How old are you anyway, Aunt Bertie?" asks Howie.

Aunt Bertie is kneading the ingredients for

her birthday strudel dough into a soft ball. "Well," she says, "I was born twenty-nine years after the assassination of Lincoln. Figure it out yourself."

Howie frowns. "That's too hard for me," he says.

"Easy for me," says Irene, writing down the numbers on a piece of paper. "*I* can figure out how old you are, Aunt Bertie."

"Big shot!" exclaims Willy. "You're nine. When you were five years old like Howie, you couldn't figure it out either."

"Could so!"

"Could not!"

"Stop arguing," says Aunt Bertie. "Both of you help your cousin Howie with the math."

Aunt Bertie herself isn't young, but she isn't old. She sure doesn't look like a grandfather's sister. Irene, Willy, and Howie think she is more up-to-date than all their other relatives. She has pointy red fingernails and wears sparkly eyeglasses with rhinestones. She has a nine-to-five job as a bookkeeper. After work she likes to play poker or dance the jitterbug. Then she drives home in her pink Chevy convertible to watch television—the first television set on the whole block.

There is only one old-fashioned thing about Aunt Bertie and that's the old-fashioned strudel she bakes.

"Now, kids, watch every single thing I do," Aunt Bertie says. Her hands move in the big bowl.

Irene is writing down the recipe on a notepad. She and the other children plan to use the recipe in the Super Strudel Factory they will build when they are older.

"How many cups of flour did you use, Aunt Bertie?" asks Irene.

Aunt Bertie stops kneading. She removes her floury glasses and wipes them with her apron.

"Let's see. I used one and a half cups, I think. Maybe a bit more. Just enough flour to hold it all together."

Now Aunt Bertie pulls down her shiny new Mixmaster from a high shelf. She plops the dough into the mixer bowl, flipping the button to On. The machine's roar fills the kitchen.

Aunt Bertie frowns. She turns off the mixer. "The old way is better," she says.

"Hooray!" the children cheer.

Slam! Then *slam!* again and again. Aunt Bertie slams the ball of dough on her metal kitchen table. She slams the dough just as her mother, Sarah, used to do.

Finally the children call out, "Ninety-nine, one hundred!" Their great-aunt lays the dough in the bowl again.

"Aunt Bertie, your swing is as good as a baseball player's," says Irene. "Better than Joe DiMaggio's." Irene is a New York Yankees fan.

Aunt Bertie laughs. She is a Brooklyn Dodgers fan herself. She often goes to Dodgers games at Ebbets Field. Sometimes she invites a lucky niece or nephew to go with her.

Irene and Willy begin to argue about which team will win the World Series.

"Dodgers!"

"Yankees!"

"Dodgers!"

"Yankees!"

"Stop arguing and get to work," says Aunt Bertie. "Help me peel the apples and crack the walnuts."

While they work, Aunt Bertie tells a story

about a boy who danced with ghosts. Later she stretches the dough over a faded old tablecloth and spreads the sweet filling over the dough. She tells another story, about a forbidden apple tree. The stories sweeten the sugar and plump the raisins. They tuck themselves between the apple slices, just as they always did.

Aunt Bertie's teakettle whistles. She gets up to pour hot water into her teacup.

"*Kinderlach*, remember to tell stories in your Super Strudel Factory," she says. "The strudel won't taste the same without the stories."

Aunt Bertie spoke Yiddish when she was a little girl. Even today she sprinkles Yiddish words like sugar in between the English ones. Especially when she has something important to say.

"When I'm the boss of my factory, there won't be any time for stories," says Willy.

Irene glares at him. "Wait a minute! It was *my* idea to have a Super Strudel Factory. I'll be the boss."

"Stop arguing," Aunt Bertie says. "You can both be a boss."

"We still won't need stories," Willy says. "That's silly."

Aunt Bertie looks sternly over her sparkly glasses at her nephew. She dunks a tea bag up and down, up and down, in her cup. "Kids, let me tell you about a strudel . . ."

Bertie's Stories

The Almost-a-Disaster Day

THIS STRUDEL WAS SO JAM-PACKED WITH STORIES,
it changed a family.

But first I have to tell you how we brought
the strudel know-how all the way from the old
country to America when I was a young girl.
And how I almost caused a disaster for everybody once we got here.

America! That's what my mother, your
great-grandma Sarah, talked about all the time,
when we were still in Odessa, Russia. By 1905,

43

my big sister, Hannah, and her husband were already here in America. From Hannah's letters it sounded as if they were living like a king and queen.

America! America has streets so clean they shine like gold in the sun, wrote Hannah. America has water flowing from silver faucets right inside your building. America has food in tins you can store on a shelf. And ice cream! I can't wait to see your faces when you taste ice cream, Hannah wrote.

America! My little brother, Abe, and I would lie in bed and talk about that faraway place. We could hear the voices of our mother and father through the wall.

"No, Sarah," said my father. "Odessa is where we stay. We have a family and friends here. I have my shop. Things are not so bad."

Night after night my brother and I listened. We could hear the low song of our mother's voice, reading Hannah's letters.

America has lights on tall poles in the street, Hannah wrote. And big buildings called public libraries, filled with books. Anyone can borrow those books. America has other buildings called public schools. Any child can study in them. Even Jewish children! For free!

My father was like a tall tree with thick roots. But my mother was the wind, soft yet strong. She could make my father bend.

Soon we heard my father say, "We will see. Maybe next year. Or maybe the year after."

Then one night my father didn't say anything at all. That was the night of a terrible uprising against the Jews in our city. A *pogrom*. My father came home with a red gash on his cheek. In his hand was one silver timepiece. That was all that was left of his watch repair shop. He sat in a chair, staring at the silver timepiece. I heard shouts outside our window. Smoke from the street filled the room, burning my eyes.

"Well, Meyer?" asked my mother.

My father took her hand.

"Sarah, children," he said at last. "We are going to America."

Now I'm getting closer to the part of the story where I almost caused a disaster for everybody.

But first let me tell you about a big good-bye party—with lots of food, and candies in little bowls. Some of our relatives had traveled from far away. I remember my uncle Yakov's beard tickling my cheek. I remember that my *bubbe*, my grandmother Leah, had a fat tear-drop trembling on her nose. Isn't that a silly thing to remember?

My *bubbe* Leah had sewn me a warm coat for the trip. It had a pale blue lining. For the sky, she said. "The very same sky covering us all, wherever we are," said my grandmother.

I remember that my mother baked a strudel for the trip. And also one hundred *kuchlech*, large diamond-shaped wafers made of flour, sugar, and water. When it was time to leave, my brothers and I carried our sacks of clothes. My parents carried a wicker trunk and bundles on their backs. What things did they choose to bring to their new home? Feather pillows. Pots and dishes. Sabbath candlesticks. The tablecloth for strudel. Yes, yes, this very cloth on my table today.

And I remember the clatter of the trains we

rode. "But where is the sea?" I finally asked. I thought we had been traveling much too long.

"We are taking the long way to the sea," my mother said. "We don't want to meet any Russian guards. They want to take Isaac for their troops."

Abe and I began to laugh. *Hoo, hoo! Ha, ha!* Our skinny brother, Isaac, with his squeaky voice and jumping Adam's apple, a soldier! He was only sixteen.

"Quiet, noodle heads," said Isaac, pinching us both.

But I remember that Isaac's eyes looked scared. That's when I began to get scared too. And because of that, I almost ruined things for everyone, as you will see.

When we stepped off that train, a stranger with a wispy beard met us. My father paid him some rubles to help us escape into Austria. We followed him through an icy river, up to our knees. We raced like rats in the night across a field.

At last we came to a small, dark house, where we all slept together in one bed.

"Is this America?" asked my little brother, Abe.

"Don't be silly, noodle head," I said, holding him close.

Days went by. It is all a blur now. There were other trains and other beds. At last one day our mother said to us, "Come, children. The big ship is here to take us to America."

I remember that ship. Its name was the S.S. *Graf Waldersee*. We sailed for twenty-three days. I was sick for all twenty-three of them. My stomach was like a storm at sea. I threw up everything, even my mother's *kuchlech*. And the smell of that ship. *Pee-yoo!* Kids, imagine all the worst smells in the world mixed up together in one big room below the deck. Rotting food, tar, waste, vomit, sweat. These smells clung to us like an invisible coat we could not peel off.

At last, like in the stories of Noah's ark and the voyages of Columbus, a seagull flew near our ship. Land was near.

"America!" Isaac shouted.

Then there was a rushing about like you never saw. My mother quickly wiped our faces with salt water. We all changed into our best clothes for our first day in the new country. It was not a cold day, I remember. Still, I put on my new coat, the one your great-great-grandmother, my *bubbe* Leah, had sewn. I was so weak I could hardly button it.

I remember the screech and lurch of the ship at the harbor. I remember the crush of the crowd on the steerage deck.

"Look!" my mother suddenly exclaimed. On our left was the Statue of Liberty, just like the pictures in books.

And just beyond the statue, I saw it. Oh, how terrifying! Something that had poisoned my dreams for a long, long time.

Ellis Island.

What awful stories we had heard about Ellis Island! It was called the Island of Tears. And not for nothing, let me tell you! They marched you into a room bigger than a marketplace, people said. Doctors poked you and asked questions. They turned your eyes almost inside out with a buttonhook, looking for problems. If they found something wrong, well, they put a chalk mark on your coat. Then back you went across the ocean. All by yourself, without your family!

Okay, kids, here comes that part of the story where I almost caused a disaster. As soon as I saw Ellis Island, I—a great big girl of eleven—became a sniffling, shivering coward. What if they found something wrong with *me*?

The guards herded us off the ship. We stepped onto the ferry. Push, stumble, hurry up, hurry up!

My family marched straight ahead. I crept behind them. My chin trembled in terror. The closer we got to the Island of Tears, the more scared I got. Even little Abe was braver than I was.

Off the ferry. Onto dry land, the ground still swaying under my feet. Into a big red building. Push, stumble, hurry up, hurry up! Down a dark hallway, holding my mother's hand. Tripping, falling. Up, up, up the steep stairs.

At the top of the stairs, the sun sparkled through great arched windows. Yes, it was the big room I had heard about. It held what seemed like one thousand people, speaking one thousand languages at once.

And yes, there they were. The doctors. The same ones from those terrible stories. They were dressed like soldiers, in blue uniforms and caps. One doctor spoke to me. As we shuffled toward him, his mouth moved. His mustache twitched. What was he saying? I was so scared I could barely hear him.

"*Blah? Blah, blabbity, blah?*" asked the doctor. He frowned and peered at me.

I could not understand him.

"Listen carefully," Papa whispered. "He is speaking our language. Answer him."

I listened carefully. The doctor was speaking Yiddish. His voice was stern. "What is your name?" he was asking.

My name. What was my name? Kids, believe me, I had forgotten.

My brother Isaac poked me, hard, in the ribs. Suddenly I remembered. Bertha. But still I couldn't answer. My tongue was a stone in my mouth. And if I opened my mouth, I knew I'd throw up, all over my new coat. All over the doctor's uniform!

The doctor reached for his chalk. He placed a big white X on my lapel. X for feeble-minded. X for send this child back—across the stormy ocean. Send her alone without her family, in the ship with the terrible smell. My parent's faces turned almost as white as that chalk. My big brother, Isaac, began to cry.

But not me. No, sir. I got spitting mad. Angry at myself, angry at the doctor, angry at everyone who had made us leave our home and family. This anger made me brave.

"My name is Bertha," I said.

But it was too late.

"Move on, move on," said the doctor, waving his hand impatiently. "Someone else will decide."

So what did I do? Kids, I wasn't taking any chances. We had suffered too much to come to this country. Here we would stay, I vowed, our whole family together.

As we walked slowly to the next group of doctors, I took off my coat. I turned it inside-out, hiding that ugly X. I put it on again. Then I walked with my family to freedom, my coat as blue as the American sky.

I've never again forgotten my name—or lost my tongue. After that day, my family said, I just talked nonstop.

The Best Gift in America

HAVE YOU EVER LAUGHED AND CRIED AT the same time? That's what we did when we saw my big sister, Hannah, and her husband, Ben, waiting for us when we got off the ferry in Manhattan. We couldn't stop hugging each other. It was hard to believe we were all together again.

It was also hard to believe what Hannah was wearing on her head.

"Is that a hat?" I asked her.

If it was, it was the biggest I'd ever seen. It had feathers and lace and ribbons of purple and yellow. Kids, if a bird had peeped out from those plumes and flown away, I wouldn't have been surprised.

"Of course it's a hat, silly," said Hannah. "This is what we wear in America."

My father looked around. *"Di Goldene Medina,"* he said. The Golden Land. "So where are the golden streets?"

We were trudging on foot to our new home, carrying our bundles.

"Maybe I exaggerated a little bit, Papa," said Hannah. "But I wanted you to come."

It wasn't only that Hannah had exaggerated in her letters. She'd also left out quite a bit.

America! She didn't tell us about the cold-water tenement we would live in, three dark rooms with soot on every ceiling. All the apartments were so close together you could shake hands with your next-door neighbor through the window. And Hannah didn't tell us about the two tiny water closets on each floor. That's where you used the toilets which you had to share with many families. She didn't tell us about the garbage dropping from windows. Or the rats in the alleys, as big as dogs. Or the odors everywhere you went. *Pee-yoo!* As bad as the smell of the ship.

On steamy summer nights, we slept on the roof. In the winter, I shivered in my "bed"—four chairs pushed together. I shared a room with my brothers.

Gray, black, and brown were the colors of our noisy, dirty neighborhood. We missed the green of Odessa and its flowering chestnut trees. We missed our sunny apartment with its featherbeds and soft velvet drapes at the windows.

But, kids, you want to know something? I loved America. It was just grand! Why? For two main reasons.

The most important reason was my best friend, Jenny. Jenny Penenny, I called her.

I met Jenny my second day. She leaned out her next-door apartment window.

"Hello, new girl," she said. "Come over. Me and my brother, Zecky, want to show you something."

She spoke Yiddish, like me. Remember, that was the only language I knew at that time.

I went over to her apartment. In Jenny's kitchen, lying on a plate, was something curved and yellow white.

"Try it," Jenny said. She pointed to the fork and knife beside the plate. "Cut it up. It's called a penenna. Eat it with some salt and pepper."

So I did. Well, Jenny and Zecky almost killed themselves laughing.

"What a greener!" they shrieked. "Cutting up

a penenna with a fork and knife! Eating it with salt and pepper!"

Can you guess what it was? Yes, I was eating a banana, for the very first time in my whole life. *Penenna* was the way Jenny pronounced it with her Yiddish accent. Jenny and her brother liked to play that trick on people who had just got off the boat. Greeners, or greenhorns—that's what they called us.

I stuck out my tongue at Jenny and ran home, bawling. But I soon forgave her. She taught me lots of games, like potsie—hopscotch to you—and how to sew rag bags filled with cherry pits to toss around. She knew about jumping into the big fountain in the square and about chasing the ambulances, just like the boys did. She was the first one to call me Bertie. I didn't mind. I called her Jenny Penenny.

Well, I sure didn't want to be a greenhorn anymore. I wanted to be a real American, just like Jenny Penenny. She and her family had come from Russia three whole years before us.

In Jenny Penenny's house they ate salad with their meal, on a separate plate. A ketchup bottle stood on the table.

In my house all the food was dumped on one plate only. And my mother said, "Lettuce is for cows, and ketchup is to cover up bad cooking."

Jenny Penenny's father had clean-shaven cheeks. He wore shiny low shoes. Oh, how young and up-to-date he looked! And Jenny Penenny's father went to baseball games.

My father had a big curly beard. I secretly wished he would shave it off. My father still wore his tall boots from the old country. And he wasn't interested in baseball one bit.

"Hmmpf!" he would say. "A waste of time, baseball. Grown men running around for no reason."

"For no reason! There sure *is* a reason," Jenny Penenny explained patiently to my papa. "The baseball players run around to get a run. To win the game!"

Jenny Penenny knew every single thing about America, I thought.

The other reason I adored America was because of my public school. So different from Odessa. It was a big building where all children—even Jewish children—could go, just as Hannah had promised. No fancy tests to see if you were smart enough, no fees, no nothing! You just skipped right through the door.

Jenny Penenny's silly brother, Zecky, almost got me in big trouble on my very first school day. Remember, I couldn't speak any English at all, so at first I was put in a special class with newcomers. But Zecky said he would teach me English.

"Bertha, when you get to class," he said, speaking Yiddish, "here are the English words you say to your teacher. Repeat after me: 'Good morning, teacher.' "

"Good morning, teacher," I repeated.

"Teacher, you have a nose like a pickle and you smell like a horse."

"Teacher, you have a nose like a pickle and you smell like a horse."

Thank goodness for Jenny Penenny! "Don't listen to him," she told me. She bopped Zecky on the head. Then she explained what I'd almost said.

My teacher, Miss O'Neill, did *not* smell like a horse. She smelled like all the flowers of the world in a beautiful bouquet. Even her hair smelled nice—a puffy pompadour.

Miss O'Neill was a very good teacher. After only one week I knew the Pledge of Allegiance. After one month I could speak English almost as well as Jenny Penenny.

"My, my, what a good student you are, Bertha!" Miss O'Neill would say.

Soon I knew all about Thanksgiving and the Declaration of Independence and the American presidents and heroes. With his beard, my papa looked a lot like Abraham Lincoln, I realized.

Sometimes Miss O'Neill ate her lunch with us in the classroom. We kids brought big meat sandwiches made with black bread and wrapped in newspaper. Miss O'Neill brought jam sandwiches made with store-bought white bread. They were cut into little squares and wrapped in a white handkerchief. American sandwiches. I thought they were the prettiest sandwiches I'd ever seen.

Miss O'Neill told us that every single one of us had sailed on a boat to come to this country. So had James O'Neill, her own grandfather, before she was born.

I stared at the big globe across the room. I

imagined boats sailing over the seas from all directions—north, south, west, and east—heading right toward Miss O'Neill's classroom.

Oh, how I loved Miss O'Neill!

In early December Jenny Penenny said, "I'm buying my teacher some beautiful soap for her Christmas gift. Or maybe I'll buy her some perfume. How about you, Bertie?"

Christmas gift! What did I know about Christmas gifts?

"Um, maybe some perfume," I said.

Jenny Penenny nodded her head in approval. "Teachers in America love gifts that smell good," she said.

We went to the drugstore to look around. Zecky went with us, I remember. It was the most beautiful store I had ever seen. I blinked when I entered. The mirrors, the lamps, the soda fountain, the tile floor—everything shone.

And there they were, little bottles of perfume lined up inside a glass case like beautiful jewels. Magnolia Dream. Splendor of Rose. Lilac Cascade. The cheapest was Magnolia Dream. It cost twenty cents—a fortune then.

"Hey, how 'bout getting her some wart remover?" Zecky said in a loud voice. "It's only ten cents. Or maybe a cigar."

That's when the frowning storekeeper came over and said, "Come on, kids, outta here!"

And Jenny replied, "We're real customers, mister. We'll be back. You'll see."

But where would I get the money for such an expensive gift? I thought and thought, and soon I had an idea.

Every Tuesday evening Mama wrote letters to the old country for our neighbors. They could speak Yiddish, but many could not write it. She charged three cents for every letter. Mama had beautiful handwriting. So did I. I asked her if I could write letters for our neighbors, too. Mama knew I was saving for Miss O'Neill's Christmas gift. She said yes, and let me keep one penny for every two letters I wrote. Kids, do the arithmetic. Figure out how many letters I needed to write.

The neighbors sat in our kitchen and waited their turn. Then each would tell me what to write in their letter.

"Tell my sister, 'The streets are so clean, you can see your face.' "

"Write, 'Mama, I will be a rich man in America very soon. Then I will send for you.' "

"Ask my wife, 'How are the children?' And tell her, 'God willing, we will all be together. I am putting aside ten dollars more for the tickets.' "

The overhead lightbulb was not very bright. The shadows made me squint. Blisters formed on my fingers.

One morning my mother said, "I have a wonderful idea. Why don't you use your pennies to buy apples on Hester Street? Together we will bake an apple strudel for your teacher."

"No, Mama," I said. "I want to buy perfume for Miss O'Neill."

"But maybe your teacher would like something tasty, something from our old home?" Mama suggested.

I shook my head. "That's not what they give teachers here in America. Jenny says the best gift is store-bought. I would be ashamed to give Miss O'Neill our plain old strudel."

Mama shrugged. There was hurt in her eyes. On the last day of school before the holiday, Miss O'Neill's desk was piled high with gifts. Thirteen bars of scented soap. Ten bottles of toilet water and cheap perfume. Buried under that pile was my Magnolia Dream.

Miss O'Neill also received a noodle kugel, one dozen cannoli, and a fruitcake.

"M-m-m-m. Home-baked. How special!" said Miss O'Neill. The children who had brought the food beamed with pride.

Suddenly I remembered how good our strudel always tasted.

"Miss O'Neill, when is your birthday?" I asked.

"Three days after President Washington's birthday, plus one," she said.

Can you guess what I gave her when her birthday came around?

"Best in America! Better than store-bought!" said Miss O'Neill when she'd tasted my gift.

Baby Lily

CAN YOU ALSO GUESS THAT MY PARENTS DIDN'T love America as much as I did?

My papa would say, "Here in America, they smile with their teeth but not their eyes."

What did Papa mean? I wondered. I began observing teeth and eyes.

My sister, Hannah, and her husband, Ben, smiled with both their teeth and their eyes, especially when their eyes looked into each other's.

My best friend Jenny Penenny's eyes were merry almost all the time, except when they had the look of terror during spelling bees. Jenny Penenny couldn't spell for beans.

During dinner, our boarder, Rosie, grinned with her eyes, her teeth, her entire skinny body. Rosie always contributed one quarter of a chicken to the soup. "Ah, good!" she'd sigh, slurping up her portion. That was practically the only time I saw Rosie awake. She was always bone-tired, working long hours in a factory—

even longer than Mama and Hannah—sewing shirtwaists. Jeepers, could she ever snore at night! I was not brokenhearted when she left to get married.

Yes, it was true that as some shopkeepers pushed their wares, their eyes didn't match their grins. But hadn't that been the case in Russia too? And what about Mr. Sullivan, the candy-store man, who gave us a peppermint for every A we got on our report cards? Even for a B sometimes. He smiled with both his teeth and his eyes.

And then there were Mama and Papa themselves. It would have been disrespectful to say, "Papa, Mama, sometimes you too smile only with your teeth." But it would have been true.

Occasionally while Mama was sewing and humming an old song, tears would drop into her lap. "What's wrong?" my brother Abe and I would ask.

Mama would look up and smile, her eyes sad. "Nothing, nothing," she'd say. But we knew she missed her own mama, far away.

Teeth and eyes, teeth and eyes.

One Sunday Papa took us to a park, a patch

of green he'd discovered several blocks away from our street. Nearby, a big sign said KEEP OFF THE GRASS. That sign was ignored, not only by us but by all the other families sharing their picnic lunches. Papa began throwing a ball to Abe. Isaac played his harmonica. I had my nose in a book. My mama, I remember, just sat, pregnant with my sister Lily. For once, her hands were still.

From the street, a tall boy approached.

"Hey, greener!" he yelled at my father. The boy pointed to the sign on the grass. "Greener, can't you read?"

Of course my father could read. Not much English, that was true. But Papa read the *Forward*, a Jewish newspaper, all the time. He was a fine Hebrew scholar as well. I wanted Papa to tell the rude boy that. I wanted him to shout to the whole world, "I may work with my hands by day fixing watches, but at night I am a scholar." Then I wanted Papa to say, "Young fellow, you are standing on the grass yourself."

Instead, Papa smiled, but only with his teeth. "Let's go home now, children," he said.

I tried not to notice my parents' eyes, scared and lost. Kids, I still loved America. I was happy. There was tag in the streets, and sometimes some licorice candy. There were fire engines to chase and the fountain at Rutgers Square to splash in. There was school, and Jenny Penenny.

Even though we were crowded into one small apartment, it began to seem as if my parents lived in one country and I lived in another. It was as if we were separated by a great big ocean.

In 1906, when I was twelve, my sister Lily was born. Lily, the first of our family born in America. She was named for *Bubbe* Leah, who had recently died. Lily's arrival lessened our sadness. I loved her to pieces. She had big round cheeks, as pink as posies. When I buried my nose in her neck, she smelled like a sweet garden.

"*Buh!*" Lily would say, looking up at me as if I were the queen of the whole wide world. *Buh* for Bertie. That was one of the first words she'd learned.

I pasted a drawing of the American flag on

her cradle. As I rocked her, I hummed our national anthem.

"None of your English words will have the accent of the old country," I told her.

But it was around that time that my father made the big ocean between us grow wider and deeper. One summer day he said, "Bertha, you will not go back to school in the fall. You're a big girl now. You must watch the baby and help Mama sew shirtwaists from the factory. Then, when you are fourteen, it will be your turn to work in the factory too."

"No, Papa!" I said. I began to cry.

My papa looked at me for a long time. What did he see? A girl scholar with smudged eyeglasses and black ink on her fingers. On her lap was a library book with gorgeous pictures of pyramids or glacier lakes or distant planets of the universe.

"I am sorry, Bertha. There is no other way," Papa said sadly. "You will do as I tell you."

Papa wasn't mean. In those days, for a girl to be a scholar was almost unheard of. And Papa was frightened. They needed my help. After the rent was paid, sometimes there was only enough money left over for herring and potatoes on the table, shoes for us kids, or medicine.

Medicine.

You see, we needed medicine for Baby Lily as soon as the autumn chill arrived. Shivering, she wheezed and gasped in the cold, fumy air of our rooms. The posies faded from her cheeks. We took turns getting up in the night, rocking her, warming her in our arms. In my dreams I can still hear her coughing. I can still see her eyes, big and round, asking us to make her feel better. But we could not. Neither could the medicine. One dark afternoon, Lily, the first of our family to be born in America, became the first to die.

And it was as if our mama had died too. Mama lay curled up in bed, her face to the wall. I never saw her sleep, or even cry. She just stared at something far, far away. Something only she could see.

"Mama? Mama?" my brother Abe would say over and over again while touching her hair, matted and unwashed, not like Mama's hair at all.

"Come, Sarah," Papa would tell her. "What

cannot be changed must be endured. You have other children."

But Mama did not get up very often. Sometimes she nibbled at bread or sipped some soup. Sometimes I heard her at night, pacing up and down the dark rooms.

But mostly Mama lay huddled in her bed, staring at the wall.

I hardly saw Papa or my brother Isaac that fall and winter. They scurried in and out of the house, leaving for their jobs before dawn and arriving home long after dusk.

From my window I would see Jenny Penenny go off to school with her friends, the bunch of them chattering and giggling. Then I would turn away and begin the work my mother couldn't do. I would scrub and sew and cook.

But the sadness darkening our home was like a layer of grime I could not scrub away. I thought about Lily all the time, though I never said her name out loud. The law had been laid down by Papa. "Never talk about Lily. Do nothing to upset your mama."

But how much sadder could Mama be?

After a while I noticed a terrible thing. My brother Abe had become a bad boy. He and his hooligan friends ran around the streets—sometimes even to the Bowery, the neighborhood where criminals prowled. They chased ambulances, hung on to horsecars, and stole bananas from market stalls. I even caught him playing poker for money behind the candy store.

"You'll grow up to be a gangster," I shouted at him.

"Aw, who cares?" he shouted back.

The teacher sent home a note: "Abe does not complete his schoolwork. If he's not playing pranks, he's staring out the window."

Papa gave Abe a good spanking when he read that note.

My brother shinnied up clothesline poles five stories high. One day I saw him racing from rooftop to rooftop, clambering across the deep, dark air shafts that separated the buildings.

"Get down! You could get killed!" I screamed. "I'll tell Papa!"

"So what? Tell him! Tell him!" Abe yelled down.

I did tell Papa, and Abe got spanked again.

But it was Mama Abe wanted me to tell. He wanted her to notice him like she used to, good boy or bad. By this time, Mama had taken to sitting by the window, staring out. Sometimes she picked up her sewing. That was a good sign, Papa said. She would pat our hands while we talked, but still, she wasn't the same. We missed our scolding mama, our baking mama, our mama whose sharp eyes narrowed at the ways of the world.

One day, thinking of Lily, I couldn't remember her dear, sweet face. A fear, then an anger, bubbled up inside me. I knew what I had to do. I gathered together a few coins and marched out to the street. There was Abe, playing hooky, leaping over milk cans outside a store. By his dirty ear I pulled my brother away from his rascal friends.

"Ow, ow! Where are we going?" Abe cried.

"Shopping," I muttered.

When we arrived home with our purchases, Mama was watching from her chair by the window.

Then she watched me measure the flour

and the sugar and the salt, just as I'd seen her do.

She watched me add the egg and the warm water.

She watched me knead the dough, then slam it one hundred times on the table. Gee, did that ever feel good! I slammed that dough as hard as I could. Abe got his licks in too.

Then, while the dough rested, my brother and I peeled the apples—and we did what was forbidden. We spoke about Lily. We remembered her round red cheeks, and how she crawled after Abe, and how she said *Buh!* instead of Bertie. We cried together. Mama listened. She cried too.

Then Abe and I spread out the tablecloth, this very one. I rolled the dough and began to stretch it. One big, raggedy hole formed, which got bigger and bigger.

"Wait, Bertha," Mama murmured.

She left her seat by the window and came across the room. She patched the hole. Then, slipping floured knuckles beneath the pale yellow circle, Mama showed me, gently yet firmly, how to stretch the dough.

When Papa and Isaac came home, can you imagine their surprise, opening the door to the sweet smells of strudel, and to Mama's smile?

Stories, strudel, and a family is changed.

Bertie's Recipe

For my Super Strudel Factory
Copied down by Irene from Aunt Bertie

Ingredients.

For the ~~doughy~~ dough
1½ cups flour (maybe you will need more).

1 Tb. sugar
a ting bit of salt
an egg (you beat it a little in a bowl) or water (the water is warm)

What you fill the dough with

3 pi slices of white bread. Make toast crumbs with this.
5 or 6 apples. Depends how big they are.
Peel them or chop them.
  a big handful of ~~raisins~~ raisins
A squeeze of a fresh lemon.
½ cup of sugar, or more if you like it sweet (we do).
maybe walnuts (but Dad doesn't like nuts)
a teaspoon of ~~cina cinnamon~~ cinnamon.
3 Tb. of ~~butter~~ butter (you need to melt it)

How to make the ~~dougha~~ dough

Take a big bowl and mix the flour, sugar + salt. Then you make a hole in the middle of the pile and you put in the egg + some warm water (to make ⅓ cups)
  Take the dough and slam it 100 times on the table.
Make a big ball, put in a bowl that you have oiled.
  Cover with a towel.
It needs to rest for 2 hours.

How to Make the Filling

Mix in a bowl the apples, raisins, lemon juice, seegar, nuts, ECT. (You can add other things too).

How to put together the strudel

Stretching

Put a Tablecloth (one with some sewing on it) on the table.

Sprinkle flour on it.

Roll the dough VERY THIN.

Put flour on your nuckles put your hands under and stretch. You can walk around the table to do this. You should see the sewing through the dough or even a piece of newspaper under it.

Patch up your holes. (Aunt Bertie doesn't have any but you usually do in the beginning.)

Putting on the filling

Spread a strip of filling (I measured 2 inches wide) in a row. Leave a border. Sprinkle over apples so Sprinkle with sugar + cinn. Brush with butter but leave some butter for the end. Sprinkle bread Toast crumbs on top (or even cake crumbs).

Rolling Up

Roll up the strudel.

Brush it with leftover butter.

Put on a pan which has oil on it.

Make it look like a horseshoe

45 min. 375 (or 350 if it's getting too brown)

Try not to eat it right away! It needs to rest for a while.

Call Aunt Bertie if you need help.

And tell stories.

Willy's Kitchen

*I*MAGINE A KITCHEN IN A SMALL house overlooking the Pacific Ocean. It seems like only yesterday, but it is several years ago. Grandpa Willy is about to make strudel. He's wearing an L.A. Dodgers baseball cap turned backward and a green apron that says HUG THE CHEF. He whistles as he drums on the kitchen counter with two forks. *Rat-a-tat-tat!*

Jessica, his twelve-year-old granddaughter, stares at him. She has a skeptical expression on her face.

"*You're* making strudel?" she asks. "No offense, Grandpa, but since when do you know how to make strudel?"

"Since I read a recipe in the L.A. *Times* yesterday," says Grandpa Willy, poking his head into the refrigerator. "The recipe's on my desk. Take a look at it." He emerges from the refrigerator with the butter dish. "Hey, here's a riddle for you guys. Why did the baseball player take his mitt to Venice Beach?"

"Oh, that's a hard one," says his younger granddaughter, Lori. She is eight. Riddles are her favorite kind of joke.

"Come on! Think! Why did the baseball player take his mitt to Venice Beach?"

"Do you know the answer, Jessie?" asks Lori, tugging at her big sister's sleeve.

Jessica is reading the strudel recipe. She shakes her head.

"We give up," Lori says.

Grandpa Willy's big sneakered feet do a little dance. *Slappity-tap!* He leans forward with his arm outstretched. "To catch some sun."

Lori laughs.

Jessica looks up from the recipe. "Grandpa . . . ," she says.

"Well, I think I've got everything I need now," says her grandfather. "Apples, raisins, cinnamon, butter—"

Jessica interrupts him. "Grandpa, there's not one word in this recipe about slamming the dough against the table, like you said your great-aunt Bertie and your sister Irene used to do. Or about stretching it so thin you can see the pattern of the tablecloth. What kind of strudel recipe is this?"

"Well, it's a modern one," says her grandfather. "Trust me. It'll be great. You know I make great things."

"He makes the best brownies," Lori says. "And zucchini soup, and chili too."

"That's true," Jessica admits. "But didn't you always say that no one could make strudel like your sister, Irene? Ever?"

Grandpa Willy sits down at the kitchen table and begins to pare an apple. A skinny red ribbon of peel falls into a bowl. "Yes, that's true," he says. "No one made strudel like Irene. Just like no one made strudel like Great-aunt Bertie, who taught Irene how to do it. But Irene won't be sending us her strudel anymore," he says quietly. "No more overnight express deliveries from Brooklyn to L.A. Someone has to take over her job."

"That's because Aunt Irene *died*, right?" says Lori in a loud whisper. She sits down beside her grandfather. "You know what, Grandpa? I never knew anyone who was *dead*, before."

Jessica frowns at her little sister. "Don't talk like that," she says. "You sound like a baby. It's a sad thing."

"I'm eight. I'm not a baby. And I am too sad," says Lori.

"Of course you are," says her grandfather. "We're all sad. We'll miss her."

Lori puts her face close to her grandfather's. "Your eyes look happier today."

Grandpa Willy kisses Lori's nose, then crosses his eyes. "That's because I remembered the answer to a riddle this morning."

"Oh, good! Another riddle," Lori says. "Is it 'When is a baseball like a chicken?' That's my favorite." Lori's sneakers go *slappity-tap*. Giggling, she leans forward with her arm outstretched. "When it's a foul!"

"That's a great riddle," says Grandpa Willy,

beginning to peel another apple. "But not the one I was thinking of. Here's mine: What's the most important strudel ingredient?"

"Apples!" yells Lori.

"Nope. Actually, today's chef will add a plum or two from his backyard tree, along with the apples. Guess again."

"Oh, yawn, Grandpa," says Jessica. "Now you're going to tell us it's the stories, like you always do. That's so corny."

"No corn. Strudel." Her grandfather winks.

Jessica rolls her eyes.

Grandpa Willy slices the peeled apples in the food processor. He raises his voice above the screech of the machine. "Remember when the big package would arrive from Brooklyn, and we'd wolf down Irene's strudel and I'd tell you the old stories? Didn't that make the strudel taste good? Believe me, without stories a strudel is a big fat flop."

Jessica smiles. "Come on, Grandpa," she says.

Now her grandfather carefully unrolls each layer of thin store-bought dough onto a sheet of plastic wrap and brushes the dough with melted butter, layer upon layer. Then he spreads a sweet-smelling rectangle of filling over the layers of dough and tells about arguments with his sister, Irene, and how they once planned to build a Super Strudel Factory, and how he and his friends in the neighborhood used to get into trouble. Sometimes he stops at the exciting parts of his stories, just like the old radio shows used to do.

"To be continued . . . ," he says.

"No, don't stop!" says Lori.

So Grandpa Willy usually tells his stories to the very end.

"Tell us about the baseball games," Jessica says.

"Ah, yes, the baseball games," says Grandpa Willy, rolling up the dough into a cylinder shape. "Irene and I saw some great games with Great-aunt Bertie."

"The Great Game of 1947: The first time you saw Jackie Robinson play in the major leagues; the Great Game of 1955: The Brooklyn Dodgers won the World Series against the Yankees," says Jessica, who has heard these stories before.

Her grandfather laughs. "Those were great moments, that's for sure." He shoves the pan of strudel into the hot oven.

Lori spreads her arms out wide. "Grandpa, what was the greatest moment in baseball you ever saw in your whole entire life?"

"The greatest moment? Hmmm . . ." Grandpa Willy gets up to warm his mug of coffee in the microwave. "To answer that question, first I have to tell you the story about the boy who hated strudel . . ."

Willy's Stories

The Boy Who Hated Strudel

HIS NAME WAS LEON AND HE WAS A distant cousin, fourteen years old to my twelve. This was a long time ago, in 1948, when the Los Angeles Dodgers used to be the Brooklyn Dodgers and played at Ebbets Field.

At first, when my parents told me that a boy named Leon would be living with us and sharing my room, I liked the idea. My friend Fidge shared a room with his older brother, Bill. Bill was the yo-yo champ of the block. He gave

Fidge lots of advice about yo-yos, and about other things too, like cars and girls. Even though Fidge was too young to drive and wasn't really interested in girls yet, the information was there if he needed it.

Anyway, I thought it would be nice to have Leon around. I figured I needed all the help I could get, with Old Big-Mouth Goody-Goody Irene for a sister.

I ran to the kitchen window of our apartment, the one facing the alley. I stuck out my head.

"HEY, FIDGE!" I yelled at the top of my lungs. "Guess what! I'm going to have a brother!"

Fidge's real name was Frank. All my friends had nicknames. Fidge was called Fidge because teachers were always telling him to stop fidgeting. I was called Yum because I liked to eat. Also because teachers called me Will-*yum* when they were annoyed with me. Our gang also included Skipper, Weasel, and Razz.

Fidge stuck his head out his kitchen window, which was across the alley from mine.

"Hey, Yum! A brother! No kidding!" Fidge yelled.

"No kidding!" said Mrs. Blum from her window.

"No kidding!" said Mr. Signorelli and Mrs. Sturtz and Mrs. O'Brian from their windows.

"When's the baby due?" asked Mrs. Sturtz.

Of course, by this time my mother had run into the kitchen so that she could tell the neighbors the *real* story.

The real story was that Leon was a long-lost relative from Europe who had been living in an orphanage in England since the end of World War II. His parents had died in the war, but I wasn't sure how. All my relatives in Brooklyn had had a big meeting in the back room of my uncle Moe's candy store, and they'd decided they would bring Leon over to the U.S. They'd also decided he would live with my family because we had an extra twin bed in my room. Also, Leon was only two years older than me. My parents hoped we could be friends as well as roommates. They also hoped I would learn a few things from a boy with "proper English manners." My friends and I were turning into hooligans, they said. Just because we were once caught smoking.

Okay we were also caught stealing. I'll tell you about *that* later.

Anyway, I was happy. Now I would have a brother, sort of.

Irene was happy. She planned to ask Leon all about the king and queen of England and what the royal princesses were *really* like.

My parents were happy. Leon would be good for me, they thought.

Fidge, Skipper, Weasel, and Razz were happy. Now we'd have two even stickball teams.

But nothing turned out exactly the way any of us imagined.

A few months later, on a Saturday, my father and my uncle went to the New York pier to meet Leon's boat from Europe. Leon had traveled across the Atlantic Ocean all by himself. I was impressed.

Meanwhile, at our apartment, a welcome party for Leon had already begun. Balloons were everywhere. Relatives were everywhere. They hugged and kissed and pinched kids' cheeks. The doorbell rang. More relatives poured in. More hugging, kissing, and cheek pinching.

The last time all our relatives had got together like that, when it wasn't even a holiday
like Passover or Hanukkah, was when my uncle
Hy came home from the war and we gave him a
hero's welcome. This guy Leon must be some
big deal, I thought.

My mother had opened up a giant folding
table right in the middle of the living room.
Piled on that table was so much food, I kept
checking to see if its legs were buckling.

My great-grandpa Meyer was already sitting
at the head of the table. He was dressed in the
shiny black suit and the little bow tie he always
wore for special occasions. He was ninety-four. I
was pretty sure he was the oldest man in Brooklyn.

Great-grandpa Meyer crooked a finger at me
to come closer.

"School's okay?" he asked.

"School's fine," I said in a loud voice. You
had to talk right into his ninety-four-year-old
ear for him to hear you.

Just then Old Big-Mouth Goody-Goody
Irene sauntered over.

"Hah!" she said. "Willy gets mostly C's and even some D's."

"What?" asked Great-grandpa Meyer.

Irene put her mouth to his ear. "WILLY GETS MOSTLY C'S AND EVEN SOME D'S!"

"Cheese and even some peas?" asked Great-grandpa Meyer.

"Good thing he can't hear me," said Irene. She skipped off to answer the door.

That's when Great-grandpa Meyer gave me a big old wink. What a guy! He was my favorite relative. I used to get the feeling I was his favorite relative too.

More relatives arrived. More hugging, kissing, and cheek pinching. I escaped into my bedroom and leaned out the window. Just as I'd thought, there were Fidge, Skipper, Weasel, and Razz standing on the street corner.

"Hey, Yum, did he come yet?" called Weasel.

"Nope," I said. "When he does, we'll be right down."

"Aw, we wanna play some ball before it gets dark," said Razz.

Let me tell you a little bit about stickball.

Stickball was the game my friends and I played every chance we got. It was kind of like baseball, except we played it with a hollow pink rubber ball called a Spaldeen, and a broomstick. The sewers on the street were our bases and our home plate. My uncle Moe used to give us free Spaldeens from his candy store. That made me very popular with the other guys. The brooms we usually got from Mrs. O'Brian, who bought only the very best. Actually we used to steal them from her when she left them out on her fire escape. Until Mr. O'Brian got his revenge, which I'll get to later on in this story.

Anyway, soon I saw my father's Buick turn the corner onto our street. My father and my uncle got out of the car, each carrying one of Leon's suitcases. Then Leon got out. He was very pale and very short, shorter than me and my friends. He was wearing a hat like my father sometimes wore, and a long coat. He was carrying a notebook under his arm.

Leon didn't look like any kid I'd ever seen in my life.

"This is Leon," said my father as they passed under my window.

"I know, Pop," I said. "Hi, Leon."

"How do you do?" Leon answered in a small, polite voice.

One thing about Leon, he was very polite. The relatives sat him down at the big table in front of a plate piled high with food. He didn't eat very much. But he did say please and thank you a lot.

"Delightful manners," said my mom, looking at me.

"How was your trip?" asked my uncle Moe.

"It was very pleasant indeed, thank you," Leon said.

Another thing about Leon. He talked English with a European accent, like some of my relatives. The really old ones.

"And now for a big surprise!" announced my great-aunt Bertie. "Irene has baked her very first strudel, practically all by herself. Leon, *this* you will love! The recipe comes straight from the old country."

"*Ta-dah!*" said Irene, proudly carrying out the platter with the strudel. You'd have thought she was bringing in the crown jewels or something.

All the relatives clapped.

"Guests first!" said Great-aunt Bertie. She cut Leon a big fat slice.

Leon stared at his piece of strudel. From where I was sitting, it looked as if Old Big-Mouth Goody-Goody Irene had done a pretty good job. Golden crust, juicy apples, raisins. Yup, all there. My mouth started to water.

But Leon just kept staring at the strudel. He looked paler and smaller than ever, if that was possible. Finally he whispered, "I'm sorry. I just can't eat it."

The relatives looked at one another. Then they all began talking at once, pretending nothing had happened. Somebody whisked Leon's strudel away and gave it to me. I wolfed it down.

"Not bad," I said to my sister.

"Well, he could have taken a teensy-weensy bite, just to be polite," Irene grumbled. "And I'll bet he's never even *seen* the king and queen of England."

Leon just sat there silently, staring at the tablecloth.

All of a sudden Great-grandpa Meyer stood up. Slowly he hobbled over to Leon. This was very unusual. Everyone stopped talking. Great-grandpa Meyer was usually the first to be seated at the table and the very last to get up. He took his meals very seriously. Anyway, Great-grandpa Meyer bent down, putting his arm around Leon. He began to talk to him. Leon answered.

And they were speaking Yiddish.

Wait just a minute here, I thought. Only old people spoke Yiddish. Sometimes parents did too, when they didn't want you to understand what they were saying. Yiddish was sort of like the Secret Code for older people. I didn't know any *kids* who could speak that old Jewish language.

But of course Leon was from the old country, and that's where he'd learned it. And there he was, using the Secret Code. Using the Secret Code with my favorite relative! Frankly, I was jealous.

"Leon is tired. He'd like to rest," said Great-grandpa Meyer.

"Willy, take Leon to your room so he can lie down," said my mother. "If he wants to, maybe you can listen to the radio together, quietly. And Willy, dear," my mother whispered in my ear, "please don't ask Leon to talk about what happened to him during the war."

"Why not?" I asked.

"Shhh. You'll only upset him. Just don't ask. And be nice to him."

I tried to be nice, I really did. I even offered Leon my own personal bed, the one that didn't squeak. I even bounced up and down on both beds to show him the difference.

"Oh, no," Leon said. "You keep your bed. I don't mind squeaks."

I gave Leon two drawers from my dresser and watched him unpack. He put his notebook on top of his underwear. He hung up his big overcoat in my closet.

Then I showed him my Lone Ranger atom-bomb ring.

"Pull out those red tail fins," I said. "Now peek inside and see the light from the bomb's energy."

Leon examined the ring politely.

"I got it by saving box tops from Kix cereal and sending away for it," I said.

"I see," said Leon. He didn't really seem interested.

The silence grew between us, as big as the Atlantic Ocean itself, it seemed. From the open window I could hear my friends, hollering away. The stickball game had begun without me.

"Are you a Dodgers fan?" I asked Leon. I pointed to the photos of the baseball players on my wall. Pee Wee, Rube, Cookie, and the Duke. Carl, Jackie, and the Preacher.

"Excuse me?" asked Leon.

Leon had never even heard of the Brooklyn Dodgers! I sighed. What would we ever find to talk about?

The Enemy Spy

I'M NOT REALLY SURE WHEN ALL THE KIDS began calling Leon the Enemy Spy. I think it started as a joke.

"Hey, Yum, where's your relative, the Enemy Spy?" some kid would ask.

"Ha, ha! The Enemy Spy is meeting a double agent in the park," I would answer.

You see, that's what had happened in this

movie we had seen. Two spies sat on a park bench, feeding the pigeons. They stared straight ahead, sharing top-secret information about the U.S. out of the corner of their mouths. My friends and I used to practice talking out of the corner of our mouths like that.

Maybe it was because of Leon's long coat, flapping around his ankles. The Russian spy in the movie had a coat and a funny accent sort of like Leon's. Of course, Leon wore that coat only once or twice. Then my mother bought him new American clothes.

Maybe it was because Leon stared and squinted at things for a long time, even after he got his new glasses.

Or maybe it was because of Leon's notebook, the one he carried around with him everywhere. Its pages were tattered and covered with stains.

"What're you writing in that old notebook anyway?" asked Fidge.

"I write down how Americans say things," Leon said.

"Huh?" said Weasel.

Leon explained. "When you say, 'Take it

from me,' you are not really giving me something. You are really saying, 'Please believe me.' When you say 'It's a wow!' or 'Out of this world!' you are saying that something is very nice."

"Everybody knows that," said Fidge.

"Wait a minute," said Weasel, pointing to the notebook. "What's all that stuff I see written in another language?"

Leon didn't answer. I remember him covering the foreign words with his hand. After that Leon stopped carrying around his notebook. Sometimes I saw him writing in it in bed at night.

Of course we knew that Leon wasn't a spy. But we still called him that. The Enemy Spy. For some reason, calling him the Enemy Spy made it okay not to be his friend. You see, Leon just didn't fit in. He was different from us regular guys.

It sure didn't help that Leon was terrible at stickball. He couldn't hit and he couldn't catch. We discovered that the first day he joined our game. He just stood there, squinting up at the sky. The ball sailed right over his head like a bird.

"I am so sorry," Leon said.

After that, Leon was always chosen last, if he was chosen at all. Pretty soon he stopped showing up at our games.

Also, it didn't help that all Leon's teachers thought he was the greatest. "Such a pleasure to have Leon in my classroom," one teacher wrote in a note home. "In just a few short weeks, he has progressed to the top of the class."

What a goody-goody! I thought. Just like Irene. Genius Leon and my genius sister sat for hours at the kitchen table doing their homework. Sometimes he asked Irene to help him with spelling. She never helped *me*, I thought to myself. Of course, I would never ask her. Anyway, I hated spelling. I hated math. It was too hard. I always raced through my homework lickety-split. Then I ran outside to play.

My teacher wrote my parents a note, too. It said, "Please have a talk with William. He is not finishing his homework. And there is too much monkey business with Frank Pinelli and others in their group."

I started having mean thoughts about Leon. Leon should go live with other relatives. Maybe he should just go back to Europe. He'd fit in better over there.

One day Great-grandpa Meyer came to visit. Leon and he talked in Yiddish, the Secret Code. Leon spoke loudly into his ear. I was sure he was telling on me. How I pretended not to see him on the street, especially if I was hanging out with my friends. How I would turn my back on him and run away.

But oh, no! Not Goody-Goody Leon!

"Leon says you are a kind boy for sharing your room," said Great-grandpa Meyer.

Maybe Great-grandpa Meyer hadn't heard everything because of his hearing problem, I thought.

"Is that all he told you?" I asked.

Great-grandpa Meyer studied me. I wondered if he knew the truth.

"Leon also had questions about stickball and baseball," said Great-grandpa Meyer. "I told him you were the expert."

I felt like a crumb. A snake. A real strikeout. The nicer Leon was, the meaner I felt.

The next night we had a terrible storm. And that's when I felt the very worst of all.

You see, I heard Leon crying his eyes out. I had never heard anyone cry like that. And it was all my fault. I was the meanest person in the family. Actually, I felt like the meanest guy in the world. I had to make him stop. I just had to.

"Leon?" I whispered into the darkness. "Leon?"

The sobbing got muffled. I could tell Leon didn't want me to hear him.

"Leon, how about if I tell you about baseball?" I asked.

There was a hiccup, then silence.

"How about it, Leon?" I asked again.

"All right," he said finally.

I turned on the lamp between our beds. I got a piece of scrap paper and a pencil. I drew a map of a baseball diamond, labeling all its parts. Leon studied it carefully. I began to talk very fast, just in case he started to cry again. I told Leon how a batter gets on base and how he gets out. And I told him about fouls and bunts and grounders and how you score. Leon wrote down everything in his notebook. He just kept writing and writing, wetting the pencil with his tongue every now and then. And I was Professor Willy, yattering away. Boy, did I ever sound smart! I knew everything. I knew enough to fill a book! Leon's book, anyway.

After a while my father banged on the wall. "Pipe down!" he hollered.

So I shut off the light. Leon fell asleep first.

The next night I introduced Leon to the Brooklyn Dodgers. Their photos were tacked up all over my bedroom walls. Some on the ceiling too.

Leon repeated their names after me. I tested him. "Who's that?" "Jackie Robinson!" "And that?" "Pee Wee Reese!" And Cookie Lavagetto and Duke Snider and Rube Walker and Preacher Roe. Soon Leon knew all the Dodgers' names and nicknames. Cold.

The next night I stood on my bed with a rolled-up comic book for a microphone. I pretended I was Red Barber, the famous radio announcer for the Brooklyn Dodgers. I mimicked his Southern accent.

"This is the ole redhead, Red Barber," I said. "The ballplayers are tearing up the pea patch! Those bases are F.O.B.!"

"F.O.B.?" asked Leon.

"Full of Bums," I told him.

"Bums?" Leon asked.

"Oh, that's what we all call the Dodgers. It doesn't mean anything bad."

And then I began to tell Leon the most exciting story in the entire history of the world. At least, I thought it was at the time. The story of the 1947 World Series between the Brooklyn Dodgers and the New York Yankees. Sure, my story had a sad ending. The Dodgers lost. But what heroes! What a series! They said the Yankees would wipe us out in just four games straight. But we showed 'em! We fought the good fight, all the way to the end of game seven.

"Friends," I said, talking into my comic-book mike. "It's game four. Yankees are leading the series two games to one. Bottom half of the ninth inning. Dodgers at bat, two Dodgers on base, two men out. Score's two to one for the Yankees."

I paused. I put my lips close to my mike. "Lavagetto swings. Strike one! The crowd's going wild!"

I paused again, lowering my voice. "There's the pitch. Lavagetto swings."

Leon's eyes were wide.

I started jumping up and down on the bed, yelling at the top of my lungs. "It's off the wall for a base hit! Here comes the tying run! And here comes the winning run! Well, I'll be a suck-egg mule!"

Leon laughed. "I'll be a suck-egg mule!" he yelled, just as loudly.

Of course, my father banged on the wall like crazy. So we turned off the light and got into our beds. But this time we didn't fall asleep right away. I remember that the room was very dark. Every now and then a car's headlights swept across the bedroom walls, lighting up the Dodger photos.

That's when I started telling Leon about Jackie Robinson. How he was the first African American ever to play in the major leagues. How lots of people jeered and threw things at him, even though he was a red-hot player and could steal bases better than anyone. How some of his Dodger teammates were mean to him, and some were nice, especially that great shortstop, Pee Wee Reese. How Pee Wee would put his arm around his shoulders and show the crowd he was Jackie's friend.

Well, all of a sudden, the most amazing thing happened. I got this great idea. Well, that wasn't the amazing thing. The amazing thing was, just as I got the idea that I was going to train Leon to be the best stickball player in the neighborhood so that he'd fit in, a car went down the street. The headlights lit up Jackie Robinson's picture on the wall. And I swear, right at that moment, Jackie Robinson winked at me! So I took that as a good sign, and we got to work the next day.

The Greatest Baseball Moment Ever

IF REAL LIFE IS LIKE THE MOVIES, MY COUSIN Leon turns out to be the best stickball player in the neighborhood. Spaldeen balls fly into his mitt like magnets to iron. He swings the bat like

a natural. He runs like a pony to all the bases—
every time.

Not only that, one day a man watches our
game. "Hey, kid!" he shouts. He points his fat
cigar at Leon. "See me in a coupla years when
you're older. For the pros."

And Leon becomes a big baseball star. Fans
in the stands yell their heads off for him. We get
to watch him on Great-aunt Bertie's TV.

Well, real life isn't like the movies. This is
what really happened:

Every night in bed Leon had his nose in his
notebook, studying the rules. Every afternoon,
after our homework, Leon and I went out to the
alley alongside our apartment building. I taught
Leon everything I knew about hitting and catch-
ing and throwing. We had a good time.

"Baseball is just like math," Leon said.

"Huh?"

"You learn the rules. The rest is practice. You
would be better at math if you'd remember that."

"Hey, who's coaching who around here?" I
asked.

I told my friends, "Leon's gonna be the
greatest when I get through with him."

"Aw, we'll believe it when we see it," they said.

"Just wait," I said. "I'm the best coach around and he's gonna be terrific!"

And Leon did get better and better. After one month, I figured he was ready. Okay, maybe he wasn't the greatest. But he was still pretty good. I took him to the next game. I even brought a new ball, just for the occasion. The guys made Leon bat first, to test him out.

I put my arm around him. I said, "You can do it, Leon!"

Leon held the bat just like I'd taught him. Not too high, not too low. Remember, we're talking about a broomstick here. One of Mrs. O'Brian's brooms, stolen and sawed off at the head.

"Go, Leon!" I yelled. "Hit it all the way to the third sewer!"

Leon smiled weakly. He tossed the ball into the air and swung.

Whoosh!

"Strike one!"

Whoosh!

"Strike two!"

Leon tossed the ball for the third time. His last chance to be the greatest. *Come on, Lee-on,* I whispered.

Cra-a-ck!!!

A hit!

No, a foul. Right onto the tiny front lawn of the O'Brians' apartment building.

After that everything happened so fast, it was like a speeded-up movie. Mr. O'Brian had been peering out his window. He raced outside in his undershirt, big silver scissors gleaming in the sun. He scooped up the ball and—*snip*—that was the end of the new Spaldeen.

"Here's your ball," Mr. O'Brian hollered, tossing two pink cups into the street. "Now stay away from my wife's brooms, or it'll happen again."

All the guys crowded around me and Leon, yelling and shaking their fists.

"Leon's some ballplayer! Hah!" shouted Weasel.

"Aw, even the greatest players hit fouls," I shouted back.

"Leon stinks!"

"Throw them both off the field!"

"Enemy Spy!"

I was burning up. I rolled up my sleeves to throw a few good punches, but then I changed my mind. Instead, I put my arm around Leon's shoulders, just like Pee Wee Reese would have.

"Leon's okay, and you guys can go jump in a lake!" I said. "Come on," I told Leon, "we're getting out of here."

We were both quiet on the way home. Leon looked really down in the dumps. But I was thinking about this super-duper new idea I had.

"I'm sorry, Willy," said Leon. "Now I made things hard for you."

"Hard for *me*? Not a chance," I said. "Next time Uncle Moe brings me a new ball from his store, they'll come around." I turned toward him excitedly. "Okay, now here's my idea . . ."

I suggested to Leon that he change his name. "Change it to Jackie. That's what Jackie Robinson wanted us to do. That's why Jackie-in-the-photo winked that time."

Leon looked puzzled. "I can't do that. I can't change my name."

I started dancing in front of him on the

sidewalk. "You don't understand. I know this story . . ."

And I told him the story about poor little Eli from long ago. Eli, who had his name changed to Yakov, fooling the Angel of Death. The story I'd heard more than once from Great-aunt Bertie, when I'd helped her bake the strudel.

"So Eli has this new name, see?" I said. "And all of a sudden, like magic, he turns into a new guy. A whiz in school, strong, great in sports, all these new friends. It could happen to you, if you change your name."

Leon shook his head. "I'm Leon. The son of Samuel and Rivka. I won't change my name."

"But it's a true story," I said. "Hey, it's worth a try."

"I know that story," said Leon. "It wasn't magic. It wasn't really the new name. Yakov believed he was smart and strong, so he was."

Flabbergasted, I stopped in my tracks. "You know that story? You *know* that story?"

"Oh, yes," said Leon. "Eli, or Yakov, was my great-grandfather. I know how he danced with ghosts, and how his apple turned to gold. My mother and grandmother and aunt also told stories while they baked. Especially when they baked strudel in the long afternoons. Same family, same stories."

Then a very stupid thing popped out of my mouth, which happened to be hanging open.

"I thought you hated strudel," I said.

"I love strudel," said Leon. "But it makes me sad to eat it."

"Sad?"

Leon shrugged his shoulders.

"Oh," I said.

It had finally sunk in. I mean, *really* sunk in. Leon's whole family branch had been chopped clean off our family tree, except for one small twig.

And that was Leon.

We sat down on the stoop in front of our building. Kids were yelling in the street. Mothers called them in for lunch, but the kids were having so much fun, they didn't hear. The air felt hot and summer-sticky, promising long days of play.

But I wasn't thinking about stickball anymore. Right then and there, I asked Leon to tell me his story.

Leon's Story

WHEN LEON WAS VERY YOUNG, HE and his family lived in a small town in Poland. One day his father told him they would have to move to another country. It wasn't safe where they lived anymore, his father said. Leon didn't understand. What was so dangerous in his tiny village, with its river so shallow he could wade across? Where skinny chickens scratched and old dogs slept in the sun?

Leon's parents tried to explain. They told him about war, about soldiers fighting, about one country trying to control another. They told him about a leader named Hitler in Germany, and his Nazi party, and about Hitler's army, marching toward Poland. And they told him about Jews being killed by the Nazis, just because they were Jews. Just because Jews prayed and spoke and dressed differently than others.

And so Leon's family moved to Hungary, to the city of Budapest, where it was safe. Leon began school. He learned to speak Hungarian. He enjoyed picnics in the park and strolls along the Danube, a river much grander than the one left behind. And Leon's mother learned to bake strudel with poppy seeds, just like her Hungarian neighbors. The moist, dark filling oozed onto Leon's fingers when he took a bite. It tasted delicious.

But a terrible war was raging in Europe and beyond. One year, when Leon was ten years old, Hitler's men marched into Hungary too. Now, like all other Jews, Leon and his family were made to wear a yellow star pinned to their clothes. Jews could no longer stroll in the parks and had to sit in the very last car of the trams. Leon saw terrible things painted on buildings as he rode the tram: JEWS ARE PIGS. JEWS ARE VERMIN. Again, he didn't understand. Maybe whoever wrote those words had never truly known a Jew, Leon thought. So he held his head high when he wore his star. See? Here I am, a person like you! he wanted to shout. Not at all what you think, a roach or an ant to step on.

Leon's father was sent to work in a prison camp. Leon and his mother were ordered to move to a small apartment with other Jews. Ten people crowded into two rooms, sharing a pitcher and a bowl for washing. Each day they lined up for their loaves of bread, and a vegetable every now and then. Each day his mother added water to the soup. Leon was always hungry.

One autumn evening he and his mother left the apartment and walked for a long time. At last they reached a large gray building. "This is an orphanage," his mother said. She kissed him good-bye. That was the hardest thing of all for Leon to understand. He wasn't an orphan, he insisted. But his mother put her hands on his shoulders. "They will feed you here," she said. "I will be back when I can. Promise me you will be strong."

Leon tried to be strong, as he'd promised. When the younger children in the orphanage cried, he held their hands. He showed them how to cover their ears and sing whenever sirens howled in the streets. And when Nazi sympathizers came to the orphanage, smashing windows and doors, murdering those they found, Leon and another boy led three small children to a dark cellar. Sometimes, by night, the two boys crept from the cellar to search for food. They didn't find much. Scraps of bread, crumbling like sawdust. Turnips, hard as stone. By day, the children slept. When gunfire boomed and whistled outside and the little ones cried, the older boys told stories in the dark. Leon tried to keep track of the days, but when you can't see the sky, that's hard to do.

At last the gunfire stopped. It was quiet for many hours. Slowly the children crept up the stairs. They had hidden so long, they could hardly stand. The light hurt their eyes. Through the broken windows they saw the Russian soldiers who had liberated their city. The soldiers lifted them up, even the older children, and carried them to safety in their trucks.

That was the story Leon told me, but not all at once. Bit by bit, it all came out, often as we lay in our beds at night. I asked many questions. There were so many things neither of us understood. One night we decided that instead of wars, there should be baseball games. Countries would show up, play by the rules, and then go home. And no one would get hurt.

One night Leon told me that his parents had been killed in concentration camps. And that he didn't always keep his promise to be strong, especially at night or when it thundered outside. I told him that in my book he was a hero.

"Stop pestering Leon with so many questions," my mother said. "Why remember sad things?"

But Leon didn't mind my questions. I think he talked about the sad things to get to the good ones. He remembered cocoa on snowy mornings, and ice skating, and riding his bicycle on red cobblestone streets. He remembered how quickly his grandmother could clean a fish, its scales flying and sparkling like rain. He remembered his father's jokes, and how his father sometimes sneezed when he laughed. And he remembered his mother's strudel, with its sweet, black poppy seed filling. He even started eating Great-aunt Bertie's apple strudel after a while. He told her it was out of this world, almost as good as his mother's.

"*Almost* as good?" asked Great-aunt Bertie, raising her eyebrows and pretending to be annoyed. But of course she really wasn't.

Leon and I did more than talk and eat strudel that summer. We played stickball. I was right about the Spaldeens, you see. As soon as I got a couple of new balls from my uncle Moe, the guys let me play. That meant they had to let Leon play too, if I had anything to say about it. Leon had good ball days and bad ball days, just like everyone else on the team.

But I still haven't told you about the greatest baseball moment ever, one shining moment I will never forget.

It happened on my birthday. That was the birthday Irene got me a Roy Rogers sterling-silver saddle ring. I still have it. Good old Irene.

And that was the birthday Great-aunt Bertie invited a whole bunch of us to a game at Ebbets Field. Her treat. We had great seats behind third base, right over the Dodger dugout.

Jackie Robinson was up. He swung the bat. A hit!

No! A foul. The ball flew toward the stands, everyone cheering like crazy. All of us reached up to that blue, blue sky, so bright and blue you could hardly see the ball—and Leon caught it.

GRANDPA WILLY STOPS TALKING, then leans back in his chair. *Ping!* goes the timer, breaking the silence. He grabs an oven mitt and opens the oven door.

"Looks good," he says. "Can't wait to prove it's just as good as the old-fashioned kind." He places the pan on a rack to cool.

"Smells good, too," says Lori. "I think *we* should open a Super Strudel Factory, Grandpa."

Her grandfather puts his arm around her and kisses the top of her head. "It's never too late," he says.

Jessica, sitting at the kitchen desk, thoughtfully taps her pencil on a piece of paper. She has drawn a family tree, its branches spreading wide across the page.

"Leon is your cousin who moved to Israel, right?" she asks.

"That's right. He has three grown children and five grandchildren."

Jessica slides her paper closer. "What are their names?"

Now, imagine this. Floating up through the sweet strudel layers, the hot steam whispers, like voices across time. *Tell our stories*, the voices say. *Tell how we swam a river, told a joke, held a baby, made a friend. Tell our stories and we will never leave you.*

Willy and Jessica's Recipe

APPLE STRUDEL

Or more!

1 (1-pound) package filo dough
2 tablespoons raisins
2 tablespoons chopped blanched almonds
1 tablespoon sugar
1/4 teaspoon ground cinnamon
Dash ground nutmeg
Toasted bread crumbs
2 medium apples, thinly sliced
1/2 cup melted butter

I like more sugar (½ c.)

If filo dough is frozen, thaw overnight in refrigerator. Remove from refrigerator 2 hours before beginning preparation, but leave package closed.

4 apples are not too many

Can use plums or pears, too

Cut 2 (26-inch) lengths of wax paper. Overlap long sides of wax paper about 1/2 inch and tape together. Using ruler and end of sharp skewer, draw 18-inch square in center of wax paper to use as template. Set aside.

Combine raisins, almonds, sugar, cinnamon, nutmeg, salt and 2 tablespoons bread crumbs in medium bowl. Add apples and toss until slices are evenly coated. Set aside.

Add some lemon zest (1 tsp.) to the filling.

Open filo dough. Unroll carefully on sheet of wax paper or plastic wrap. Separate half of sheets, re-roll in plastic wrap and refrigerate or refreeze for another use.

Cover remaining half filo with sheet of wax paper or plastic wrap, then damp towel, to prevent drying. Towel should not touch dough.

Place 2 sheets filo, overlapping enough to form 18-inch square, on template. Brush with melted butter and sprinkle with scant tablespoon of bread crumbs.

Layer remaining filo, 2 sheets at a time, alternating directions. Brush each layer with butter and sprinkle with bread crumbs.

Place filling in 12x4-inch rectangle about 3 inches from 1 edge of dough. Using wax paper to lift dough, fold in sides.

Beginning at end near filling, roll filo jellyroll fashion, encasing filling. Continue to roll, lifting dough with wax paper.

Place roll seam-side down on greased jellyroll pan. Brush with melted butter. Bake at 375 degrees 25 to 30 minutes, or until golden brown.

Remove from oven and cool in jellyroll pan on wire rack about 30 minutes. Slice strudel diagonally. Serve warm or cold. Makes 8 to 10 servings.

From the L. A. Times

Short-cut strudel but still good!

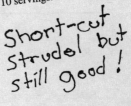

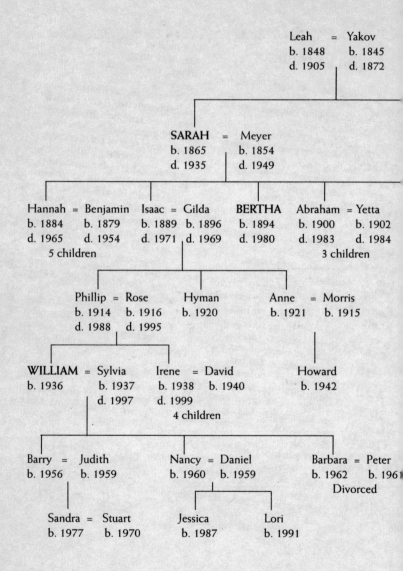

The Strudel Makers

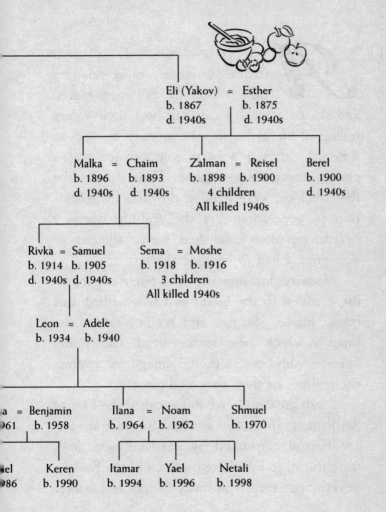

Eli (Yakov) = Esther
b. 1867   b. 1875
d. 1940s   d. 1940s

Malka = Chaim   Zalman = Reisel   Berel
b. 1896   b. 1893   b. 1898   b. 1900   b. 1900
d. 1940s   d. 1940s   4 children   d. 1940s
                   All killed 1940s

Rivka = Samuel   Sema = Moshe
b. 1914   b. 1905   b. 1918   b. 1916
d. 1940s   d. 1940s   3 children
             All killed 1940s

Leon = Adele
b. 1934   b. 1940

a = Benjamin   Ilana = Noam   Shmuel
061   b. 1958   b. 1964   b. 1962   b. 1970

iel   Keren   Itamar   Yael   Netali
986   b. 1990   b. 1994   b. 1996   b. 1998

Author's Note

AS A YOUNG GIRL, I LISTENED to the stories my older relatives told, especially as we prepared and shared a meal. I can still hear their voices telling of life in Russia, the journey by ship to America carrying a brass samovar for tea, a child's illness, a street game. Their stories, like their recipes, were handed down from generation to generation. Yet the real-life stories I heard were often unfinished, mere fragments of memories. I had to imagine the rest.

Memory. Imagination. And one more ingredient added to the blend as I was writing this book: history. Stories and recipes reflect the times in which their creators lived. The strudel bakers in this book, although imaginary, express the realities of their time and place.

Sarah grew up in what was called the Pale of Settlement, an area in western Russia and eastern Poland controlled by czarist Russia. Jews were forced to live there by order of the Russian government, mainly in small villages and market towns. Jews could not own land. Most made a poor living as tradespeople and artisans, exchanging goods with the peasant farmers who lived nearby.

A family's primary pleasures were derived from the observance of the Sabbath and holidays and, for the boys and men, intense religious study. As Sarah tells us, girls were taught in the Yiddish language, once considered inferior to Hebrew, the language of the holy books. Yiddish was the language all eastern European Jews spoke for hundreds of years in their daily lives, in time producing a great legacy of Yiddish literature, poetry, and philosophy.

Russian officials often spoke of "the Jewish problem": what to do with these strange outsiders, a people with their own language, customs, and religion who would not convert to Christianity. They tried to force the Jews to attend nonreligious schools. Jewish men were conscripted into the army, where they were often mistreated and forced to abandon their beliefs. During the reign of Czar Alexander III (1881–1894), the situation worsened. At that time a bright Jewish student like Eli/Yakov, perhaps desiring to broaden his education, to travel, or to acquire a profession, would have been greatly restricted from doing so. Mobs of non-Jewish peasants, hungry and oppressed themselves, were encouraged by government agents to blame their difficulties on the Jews, rather than on the corrupt and inefficient people in power. This resulted in the violent attacks called *pogroms*, and the decision by the fictional Bertie and her parents, like my ancestors, to join the millions from around the world seeking a better life in America.

Was it a better life? Was it worth that terrible journey by ship? It depends who was telling the story. Certainly a crowded urban area like the Lower East Side of New York, where Bertie's family lived, was no paradise at the turn of the century. As in the old country, poverty was the norm. People worked long hours for little pay. Children often helped out at home by doing piecework from factories, many leaving school at fourteen to join the workforce themselves. And 1906 was the height of the tuberculosis epidemic in that city. Thousands of children, like the infant Lily, did not survive the harsh conditions.

Still, as Bertie's older sister, Hannah, had promised in her letters, America offered freedoms and delights Bertie had never experienced, especially with regard to her education. To think and talk and look like an American became the goal for most immigrants, not only those from eastern Europe. Two generations later, Willy, the assimilated grandchild of immigrants, considered the Yiddish language merely a "secret code" spoken by parents and grandparents.

For many newcomers, baseball was the ultimate American sport. Yet baseball manifested a negative aspect of American society: segregation. The game was not integrated until 1947, when Jackie Robinson, to much protest, joined the Brooklyn Dodgers. And the fear of communism after World War II had created a growing climate of distrust toward anybody considered un-American. Enter my character, Leon, a war refugee shunned by the other children because he was different. Leon was a survivor of the Holocaust, the horrific culmination of the search for a solution to "the Jewish problem" in Europe.

During my historical review, I was greatly moved by the memoirs of ordinary people. Their individual voices spoke across the boundaries of place, time, and custom to reveal our common humanity.

And that, for me, is the power of all our stories.

Joanne Rocklin

About the Author

Joanne Rocklin is the acclaimed author of more than a dozen books for children. A former elementary-school teacher and psychologist, she now writes full-time. She is a member of the Advisory Committee for the Museum of Tolerance "Once Upon a World" Storytelling Program of the Simon Wiesenthal Center in Los Angeles and is a founding member of the outreach organization California Readers. Originally from Montreal, Joanne Rocklin has two grown sons and lives in Los Angeles with her husband, Gerry, and three cats.